My Book

by Jane Belk Moncure

illustrated by Pam Peltier

THE CHILD'S WORLD

ELGIN, ILLINOIS 60120

Library of Congress Cataloging in Publication Data

Moncure, Jane Belk.
  My "u" book.

  (My first steps to reading)
  Rev. ed. of: My "u" sound box. © 1984.
  Summary: Little "u" fills her box with umbrellas and
many other things that begin with the short letter "u."
  1. Children's stories, American.   [1. Alphabet]
I. Peltier, Pam, ill.   II. Moncure, Jane Belk.   My "u"
sound box.   III. Title.   IV. Series: Moncure, Jane Belk.
My first steps to reading.
PZ7.M739Myu   1984   [E]   84-17548
ISBN 0-89565-276-5

Distributed by Childrens Press, 1224 West Van Buren Street,
Chicago, Illinois 60607.

My "u" Book

(This book uses only the short "u" sound in the story line.
Words beginning with the long "u" sound are included at
the end of the book.)

Little  had a

She said, "I will fill my

First I will find an umbrella.

I will run, run, run

to find an umbrella."

Why did Little  get under the box?

Why was the box upside down?

Little  found an umbrella.

She found lots of umbrellas.

She put one umbrella over her head. Guess what she

did with the others?

Just then the sun came out.

Little put the put the umbrella down.

But then the rain came

down again.

Little put the

umbrella up.

Then she saw some underclothes.

They were getting wet.

She took the underclothes
off the line.

She put them into her box.

Little  took the underclothes upstairs.

She put them away.

"Now I can play under my umbrella," she said.

She went out in the rain.

"I can run through a

mud puddle,"

she said. "What fun!"

Then Little u found an ugly duckling.

The ugly duckling was grumpy.

19

She put the ugly duckling

into her box.

"Do not be grumpy," she said.
"You will grow up to be beautiful."

Just then her uncle came by.

Little gave her uncle an umbrella.

Next, an umpire came by.

"Can you help us?" he said.

"We are playing baseball in the rain. We need umbrellas."

Little  said, "I have a box full of umbrellas."

She gave the umpire an umbrella.

Then she gave everyone an umbrella.

ugly
duckling

underclothes

BOX

umbrella

uncle

umpire

What fun they had in the rain.

More words with Little .

undershirt

Uncle Sam

usher

umbrella bird

umbrella tree

29

Little 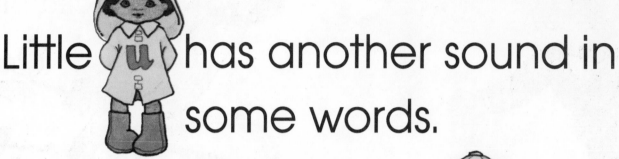 has another sound in some words.

She says her name. Listen for Little 's name

ukulele

uniform